# THE DAY CHUBBY BECAME CHARLES

# THE DAY CHUBBY BECAME CHARLES

by Achim Bröger

translated from the German
by Renée Vera Cafiero

with drawings by Emily Arnold McCully

J. B. Lippincott New York

The Day Chubby Became Charles



First published in Switzerland by Verlag Nagel & Kimche AG, Zürich,
under the title *Oma und ich*.

 Printed in
the United States of America. For information address
J. B. Lippincott Junior Books, 10 East 53rd Street,
New York, N.Y. 10022.
Typography by Patricia Tobin
10 9 8 7 6 5 4 3 2 1
First Edition

Library of Congress Cataloging-in-Publication Data
Bröger, Achim.
[Oma und ich. English]
The day Chubby became Charles / by Achim Bröger ; illustrated by Emily
Arnold McCully; translated by Renée Vera Cafiero. — 1st ed.
p. cm..
Translation of: Oma und ich.
Summary: Afraid that her grandmother might be dying, Julia
discovers a new friend with whom she can talk about her fears.
ISBN 0-397-32144-9 : $ — ISBN 0-397-32145-7 (lib. bdg.) : $
[1. Grandmothers—Fiction. 2. Friendship—Fiction. 3. Death—
Fiction.] I. McCully, Emily Arnold, ill. II. Title.
PZ7.B78618Day 1990 89-13112
[Fic]—dc20 CIP
AC

# THE DAY CHUBBY BECAME CHARLES

# Chapter One

As she did every afternoon, Julia walked along the fence with her backpack on her back and Jacob alongside her.

As always, Chubby trailed a couple of steps behind them, not saying a word.

Julia and Jacob were complaining about all the homework they had to do. "Eight problems in arithmetic. And all that reading?" Then they talked about the fistfight between two big boys from the seventh grade. "Bam, bam, bam!" Jacob punched the air, showing off for Julia.

Julia jumped to one side to avoid being hit, almost tripping over Chubby. "Why don't you watch where you're going?" she snapped. "Here, hold this a minute." She took off her backpack and handed it to Chubby. "I want to show you something Oma and I saw on TV last night." Oma was Julia's grandmother.

"What?" asked Jacob.

"Tightrope walking. They did a live show from the circus."

"I watched it too," said Jacob. "It was terrific!"

Julia balanced on the edge of the sidewalk, pretending it was the high wire. She took a careful step, setting one foot in front of the other, then another step, and another, her arms stretched out for balance. She teetered a little, but kept her balance—just a few steps more.

She made it! Julia bowed to her audience, and Jacob clapped. Chubby wanted to clap, but he couldn't because he was holding Julia's backpack. And when she took it back from him, it was too late to clap.

"That show was great," Jacob said. "Did you see the way they flew from one trapeze to the other? Doing somersaults high up in the air."

"And the way they juggle so many plates," said Julia. "My grandmother tried to do it with just one plate. She threw it high in the air, and—"

"Caught it?" asked Jacob.

"No," said Julia. "Oma isn't a juggler. Oma is Oma. It shattered into a thousand pieces all over the living room."

"That's impossible," said Jacob. "It couldn't have been more than ten."

"Well, ten is a lot," said Julia.

By this time Julia and Jacob had passed the brown fences and were approaching Julia's house. Chubby trailed behind them, not saying anything.

Julia lived in a house with a tall gray roof. Like most houses in the town, it was made of red brick. Next to the house was a big barn with a broad wooden door where the tractor and the car were usually parked.

Today Julia's father was working with the tractor in the fields, and her mother had taken the car to do the shopping.

From where she stood, Julia could see over the fence, past the big linden tree, and into the kitchen window.

Oma was always there to wave to Julia when she got home from school. Every afternoon.

But today the white curtain was drawn and the window was empty.

That was strange! Where was Oma?

Julia waved a quick good-bye to Jacob and ran across the yard.

Why is she in such a hurry all of a sudden? thought Jacob.

# Chapter Two

Julia pulled open the heavy front door leading into the gloomy hallway.

"Oma!" she yelled. She stood there and listened. Oma didn't answer. "Oma?" she called a second time, more quietly. But the house remained silent.

Julia was about to toss her backpack into the corner—*slam!*—as she usually did, just to hear Oma say, "Do I have to tell you every single day not to throw your bag around like that?" but she didn't.

The house was so strangely quiet, it was almost eerie.

Everything seemed so different. Julia ran into the kitchen.

The kitchen was empty! So were the living room and the bathroom. She ran to the basement door. It was locked. She raced back to the kitchen. On the stove was a big pot of stew.

Next to the pot was a note. Julia read it slowly:

*I don't feel well and I'm resting in my room. Warm up your food! Also, please get some things for me. The shopping list and money are on the kitchen table.*

*Love,*
*Oma*

Oma sick? She can't be sick.

The kitchen clock ticked loudly.

Julia had to see Oma right away. She had to find out what was wrong with her.

She tore open the door and ran down the hallway. Oma is sick! Oma is sick! kept going through her head. She raced upstairs to Oma's room.

Stop! She shouldn't be so noisy—Oma might be sleeping.

Julia walked quietly toward Oma's room. Oma's dark coat and her hat hung on the coatrack by Oma's door. Julia stood in front of the door and leaned forward. She held her breath and listened.

Nothing. Not a sound!

Oma must be asleep.

Julia grasped the doorknob and turned it slowly. It creaked anyway.

Oma's room was dark—the curtains were drawn.

Julia tiptoed into the room and stood there looking at the big bed.

Oma was lying on her back, not moving. She looked like—Oh . . . she couldn't be, thought Julia.

Julia forced herself to take a small step closer to the bed.

Oma looked so white, so different.

Julia felt scared. She stared at Oma.

Oma's mouth was open, her eyes closed. Her face was white, and her nose looked sharp. She was covered with a light blanket.

Then Julia noticed a funny smell in the room.

What was wrong with Oma?

Julia got more and more scared.

Only yesterday she and Oma had watched TV, and Oma had juggled a plate. Why was she lying there like that?

A bottle of medicine stood on the night table. A spoon lay next to it. That must be why the room smelled so funny—because of the medicine.

Suddenly Julia heard something. A little snore. Maybe she had imagined it?

There it was again. A very quiet snore. Julia was filled with relief.

If a person was snoring, then she had to be alive.

Snoring Oma! thought Julia. Dear snoring Oma. A warm feeling ran through Julia. She came up closer.

The label on the medicine bottle read: MA-DO-SAN FORTE. Julia had never heard of it. Madosan forte. She decided to let Oma sleep, so she went out of the room and shut the door.

On the rack hung Oma's coat. Julia sniffed it. Yes, that was what Oma smelled like when she didn't smell of medicine.

She sniffed it again. It smelled like Oma.

# Chapter Three

*Warm up your food!* the note said. The exclamation point almost ordered her to do it. Julia stood at the stove and obeyed Oma's note. But all the while she was thinking, Is Oma *very* sick?

Julia filled her plate with vegetables, potatoes, and meat. Then she sat down at the table and poked around at the plate. She wasn't a bit hungry.

Oma wanted her to get some things. The shopping list and money were on the kitchen table. *Love, Oma.* Julia shoved aside the plate. It was much too quiet in the big house with her grandmother sick upstairs.

The clock ticked loudly. Usually Julia didn't hear it because of all the different sounds and noises in the house.

Julia grabbed the pendulum. She couldn't stand the constant ticking.

Beside the clock hung her parents' wedding picture. Next to it was a photograph of Oma in a black wooden frame. In the picture Oma was sitting in a living-room chair with her knitting in her lap. Oma could never just sit doing nothing. She had never learned to be that way, she said. Julia had never learned to be that way either, but she was good at it anyway.

Oma smiled at Julia from the photograph. It was a secret smile. You had to know Oma really well to notice that smile.

"Oma, what's wrong with you?" Julia asked the picture.

Then she remembered the box in the living-room closet. It was full of photographs of Oma.

In a matter of seconds Julia was squatting in front of the box, looking at a picture of Oma and herself. Darn! She was supposed to do the shopping. And the stores would be closing soon. She would look at the pictures later.

She put the photo inside her shopping bag next to the list and her wallet. She didn't really know why she was taking it; she just felt she wanted to have it with her.

Julia stood in the hallway, looking up the stairway to the second floor and to Oma's room. Something inside her said, "Hurry, up the stairs!"

She raced up the stairs. She absolutely had to see Oma.

Oma was lying there just the way she had

before. Her nose was sharp. Her face was pale, as if she were—No, not that. Julia pushed the thought away.

She moved closer to the bed. Quietly. Very quietly. Touching the blanket, feeling it.

She wanted to touch Oma, but she didn't dare. Oma was lying there so motionless. Instead, Julia softly stroked the blanket.

Then, forgetting to be quiet, she raced down the stairs, grabbed the shopping bag, and ran out of the house. She *had* to do the shopping.

# Chapter Four

Julia came to a stop under the broad limbs of the linden tree. What was on Oma's shopping list? She didn't even know what store to go to. Milk. Six eggs. A quarter pound of liverwurst and a stick of butter. She could get all that at Mrs. Tammen's store. Oma and Mrs. Tammen were friends.

A thought crossed her mind. She could ask Mrs. Tammen what the medicine was for. Maybe she would know, and tell her what was wrong with Oma. What was the name of the medicine on Oma's night table? Madosan—that was it.

Something fell out of the linden tree, bounced on the pavement, and lay still. A cherry pit.

Julia heard a giggle from high among the branches. Jacob! she thought. It had to be Jacob. He was waiting for her to come out and play, as they often did in the afternoons. The nerve of him, throwing cherry pits at her.

Julia dropped the shopping bag and started climbing the tree. Just you wait, she thought. She saw his shoes on a thick limb a little way above.

He climbed higher, and Julia climbed after him. She knew her tree very well. She had climbed it almost to the very top at least a hundred times.

Oma used to scold her: You're worse than a boy. But Oma had gotten used to her climbing granddaughter. Julia didn't think she was worse than a boy. She could climb as well as any boy.

Julia pulled herself up to another branch, climbed up to the next, and held on tight. She gripped the branch above her. She was only inches away from the figure above her; she'd get him now. She liked Jacob. He was funny, and he talked a lot, and he was always fun, even if he did like to show off sometimes.

There were his feet. Julia grabbed him by the trouser leg and pulled. "Gotcha!" she shouted, and looked up.

It was Chubby. That's all I need! What a bore, thought Julia.

As usual, Chubby didn't say anything. He just looked down at Julia from between the branches and leaves of the linden. Julia was surprised that he had climbed up so high.

She pulled herself higher. Now she was level with him but on a different branch.

Chubby held out a cherry to her. She guessed he wanted her to eat it, but she didn't want to. She wanted to yell at him: "Hey, what are you doing in my tree?" but instead she yelled, "We don't need you snooping around, looking in our windows!"

Chubby stared at Julia, not saying anything.

Julia knew she was being mean.

What a moron! she thought. He could sit there forever, not saying a word, and become a part of the tree. Then all at once she felt sorry for him.

"Want to go shopping with me?" she asked.

Chubby nodded.

"Say *something,*" said Julia.

"Yes," said Chubby.

Oh, for goodness' sake, Julia thought, it was hardly worth opening your mouth if all you were going to say was "Yes."

Julia climbed back down, not noticing that Chubby was climbing down with her, so she was surprised when he jumped down to the ground and landed next to her at the same time. He really did know how to climb trees.

She picked up the shopping bag and looked at Chubby, wondering why he was called Chubby. He wasn't fat. Maybe a little slow, and maybe a little chunky, but fat? No.

"Are you coming?" she asked. Suddenly Julia needed to tell someone about Oma, and since no one else was there, she told Chubby. "My Oma is sick."

For a little while, when she had wanted to catch the cherry-pit thrower, Julia had almost forgotten her sharp-nosed, pale Oma. But now her thoughts were back with Oma.

"Come on, let's go, Chubby," said Julia. Chubby is a really dumb name, she thought. I'll ask him what his real name is later.

# Chapter Five

Chubby walked next to Julia, still not saying a word. Julia couldn't stand his silence, so she talked. "I have to get milk, eggs, butter, and . . . there was something else." She reached for the shopping list in her bag. As she did so, she felt Oma's photograph between her fingers.

"A quarter pound of liverwurst," she read. Chubby nodded, as if he already knew that.

But he couldn't have known, thought Julia.

"So what's your real name?" she asked. "Chubby—what a silly name. I wouldn't want to walk around with a name like that."

Chubby looked at Julia with surprise.

"My real name? It's . . . Charles," he said. His eyes seemed happy.

Julia said, "So that's your name!"

He nodded.

There were two bicycles in the bike stand in front of the store, and there were posters in the store window.

"Wait here," said Julia. She didn't want Charles to be with her inside the store. She had to be alone when she talked with Mrs. Tammen about her grandmother.

The bell on the door jingled. Three heads turned toward Julia. There were two customers, and Mrs. Tammen was standing behind the counter cutting a loaf of bread.

"Hello," said Julia.

"Hello, Julia," Mrs. Tammen replied.

Julia wanted to talk to Mrs. Tammen alone.

It took forever for the first customer to finish her shopping. She squeezed oranges and asked if the bread was really fresh. Mrs. Tammen answered her patiently while Julia got more and more impatient.

Was Chubby—Charles—still waiting outside? Julia wondered. She looked out the window between the posters. He was there, standing by the bicycles.

Finally the first customer left and it was the second one's turn. *Madosan forte, Madosan forte* went around and around in Julia's head.

Fortunately the other woman was faster. Now Julia was alone with Mrs. Tammen. "Well?" she said, putting her hands on her hips and looking at Julia through her thick lenses. "What do you need?"

"Liverwurst, a quarter pound. Six eggs. A stick of butter—"

"Anything else?"

Julia wanted to tell her about Oma, the way she was lying in bed, and ask her about the medicine. But she didn't know how to start. Mrs. Tammen looked so forbidding.

Julia couldn't bring herself to ask anything.

"Well, what else?"

"A quart of milk," said Julia. The milk appeared in front of her.

"And?" asked Mrs. Tammen. "Hurry up, child, I have to close up."

"Two rolls," said Julia. Oma hadn't written that on the list. Julia asked for them because she didn't want to leave. "And a bar of milk chocolate," she added.

Now it was all in her shopping bag, but Julia didn't say anything and didn't leave. She stood there, dumb—almost like Charles. "Oma is sick," she finally blurted out.

"What's wrong with her?"

"I don't know."

"Is she in bed?"

Julia nodded. "She's just lying in her bed, not saying anything," she said.

"She's probably asleep. And where are your parents?"

"Daddy is somewhere in the fields, and Mama is in the city."

"Your mother must have gone shopping. People come in here only when they forget to buy something in the city. Oh, well, that's how it is," said Mrs. Tammen. "Listen, I'm in a hurry," she added.

"Is Oma . . ." Julia started.

The old lady waited for the rest of the sentence; then she asked, "Is Oma what?"

Julia could only look at her.

"Oh," said Mrs. Tammen, "you want to know whether your Oma will get better? You're afraid she will die?"

Julia nodded.

"No, I don't believe that for a minute,"

Mrs. Tammen said. "Your Oma's a year younger than me. She's much less wrinkled. You know, we went to school together, a long time ago. She was in here the other day, complaining that the licorice was stale. No, your grandma won't die anytime soon."

"She's taking medicine. It's called Madosan forte."

"Never heard of it," said Mrs. Tammen. "But if she has something, the doctor must have given it to her. He'll know what's wrong with her. Now, Julia, I really have to close up."

"'Bye," said Julia.

"Wait! You haven't paid for the groceries," Mrs. Tammen said.

"I forgot." Julia paid and left.

The old lady shuffled to the door and locked it behind Julia. Hmm, Charles! Mrs. Tammen said to herself. It's usually Jacob.

# Chapter Six

Charles trailed behind Julia just as he always did. Julia took no notice of him; her mind was still on Mrs. Tammen's words. Around and around they went in Julia's head: *Your grandma won't die anytime soon.*

*She* didn't see Oma lying there like that, thought Julia. Her face was so pale, her nose sharp.

Julia turned around. "Hey!" she called to Charles. "Hurry up!"

Charles took a couple of faster steps, and they walked next to each other.

"Hello, Mr. Brunner," called Julia to a thin man on a bicycle. The man waved to them and rode on.

"Mr. Brunner's pretty old," said Julia.

"Yes," said Charles.

"Can't you say anything else?" said Julia in exasperation.

"He must be fifty at least," said Charles.

"He's over seventy," said Julia. "Oma told me."

"That old!" said Charles. "And he still rides a bike."

"I suppose you think that's something you can't do when you're real old," said Julia. Then she said, "My Oma is old."

"Grandmothers are always old," said Charles.

"No," she said. "Oma doesn't feel she is old."

"How do you know that?" Charles asked.

"She told me. She said something else, too."

"What?"

Julia stopped. She wanted to repeat exactly what Oma had said. Then she spoke, slowly and hesitantly. "Oma said some people get old very early, as if they've always been old. They aren't interested in anything. All they do is complain. There are other people, Oma said, who you realize are old only when they die. You don't realize this before—like with Oma."

"But she isn't old," said Charles. "You just said so."

"Maybe now she is," said Julia. "She's sick and she's in bed. Today my Oma is different."

Charles didn't say anything. He's starting that again, thought Julia.

"You're really old when you're very sick and you're a grandmother," said Charles.

"So today Oma is old," said Julia.

"Maybe she'll die soon," Charles blurted out.

Julia could hardly breathe. Oma isn't that old, she kept telling herself.

They were approaching Jacob's house. Julia didn't want to walk by it. Jacob might see her with Chubby and think she was dumb.

No, Julia definitely didn't want Jacob to see her with Chubby. But she was annoyed with herself for being embarrassed. I can be with anyone I want to, Julia decided. And if I want to walk with Charles, that's my business.

Still she hoped Jacob wouldn't see them together.

As they walked by the garden gate, Julia

gave a sigh of relief—Jacob was nowhere to be seen.

A street led off to the right. "I live down there," Charles said, and grabbed her arm. "I want to show you something!"

"I don't have time," said Julia. "I have to get back."

Charles' shoulders sagged. "I've never shown it to anyone before," he said softly.

"And you want to show it to me?" asked Julia.

"Yes," Charles said.

Julia did want to see something nobody else had seen before. "Okay," she said, "I'll go with you. But not for long. My Oma's sick in bed."

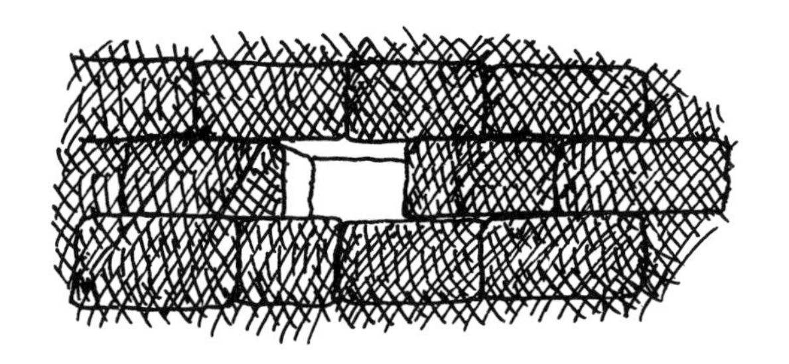

# Chapter Seven

Charles suddenly realized that he might not be able to show Julia his secret. He could only do it if his parents and his big brother weren't home.

"Wait," said Charles, and ran inside his yard. Julia waited impatiently for whatever it was that Charles had never shown anyone before.

"Come on!" Charles shouted from the front door. He led her around to the back of the house, stopped at the porch, and pointed to several bricks in the wall.

"Well, what about them?" asked Julia. Charles got down on his knees and removed a loose brick. He looked around to make sure no one was coming, took eight more bricks out of the wall, then crawled inside. A moment later his head and hand reappeared, and he beckoned to Julia.

"But it's dark in there," said Julia.

"I have a flashlight," said Charles.

Julia just *had* to see Charles' secret. She crept inside and crouched next to him in a small, low space. Charles picked up the bricks and closed the opening. Only a small chink remained open, which allowed in a little light.

Julia felt as if she were in a cave. Secret and adventurous. It was fun, but it made her a tiny bit afraid, too.

Charles shone the flashlight on everything in the room.

The cement floor was covered with old remnants of carpeting. A footstool stood in front of a plywood crate that served as a table. A couple of bricks were stacked for a second seat. There was another crate for storage, and it held all sorts of things.

"It's almost like a living room," said Julia.

"Yes, it's my secret room," said Charles softly.

He sat down on the brick chair; Julia sat opposite him on the footstool. The flashlight was next to the table.

"What a neat room!" said Julia.

"They used to hide here during the war when the bombs were coming down," Charles explained.

"It's a great hiding place," said Julia.

"And it's mine," said Charles. "Nobody knows about it now. There used to be a door leading down here from inside the house."

He aimed the flashlight at the opposite wall. "The door was right there—do you see where the stones look newer? There used to be a closet on the other side. You got to the door through the back wall of the closet that led to this room."

"That's exciting," said Julia.

"Yeah. . . . My grandfather walled it off when I was little. He said we didn't need it anymore."

"You have a grandfather?"

"He's dead."

"Are you sad that he's dead?" asked Julia.

"Sometimes I am. But mostly I'm not."

"Why not always?"

"Because I don't always think about him. That's why I can't be sad all the time. Anyway, sometimes I think about him and smile because I remember something funny he used to do."

"I know I'd think about my Oma all the time," said Julia.

"And you'd always be sad?"

"No, sometimes I'd smile too. But right after that I'd be really sad again."

"Because you'd suddenly remember that she wasn't there anymore?"

"Yes," said Julia. "I think that's how it would be."

"Same with me and my grandfather."

"Does anyone else know you can move those bricks?" asked Julia.

"No," said Charles. "Nobody!"

Julia was glad that she was the only one who knew Charles' secret. "Why didn't you show it to anyone before?"

"Because I didn't know anyone I wanted to show it to," Charles said.

Julia picked up a rag doll that was in a shoe box. "Yours?" she asked. She could see Charles' face getting red. "I have one too," said Julia. "I've had it for a long time."

"You're allowed to. You're a girl."

"And you're not supposed to?"

"My father says I'm too old for that, and besides, I'm a boy."

"So what?" said Julia. "What's the big deal anyway?"

"My father yells at me, and my brother laughs at me," said Charles.

"Is that why you hid your doll here?" asked Julia.

"Yes," said Charles. "That way nobody can say anything about it—they don't know about it."

In the box Julia also saw a baby bottle. "Was this yours?" she asked.

Charles nodded.

"Want to know something?" said Julia. "I found my old baby bottle a couple of weeks ago, and I bought a new nipple for it at Mrs. Tammen's. She wanted to know if I was going to have a new brother or sister, and I told her the nipple was for me. I put it on the bottle and drank cocoa out of it. It tasted so good. Oma laughed because I was riding around on her bicycle sucking the bottle."

Charles had to laugh, just like Oma. "Sometimes I drink out of my baby bottle too," he said, and fell silent.

They both sat for a while not saying anything. Then Charles asked, "Do you want to leave?"

"No," said Julia. She was thinking how nice it was that Charles was talking and sharing his secrets with her. She wanted to stay longer. But what if Oma needed her? No, she decided, Oma was sleeping, and all I'd be doing is sitting there alone.

Then she thought, I hope she *is* sleeping. I hope I really did hear a snore. Of course I did. Julia was pretty sure. But she wasn't *sure* sure she had heard Oma snore.

# Chapter Eight

"Do you want something to drink?" asked Charles. He picked up the baby bottle.

"Out of that?" asked Julia. Charles nodded.

"Okay," said Julia.

"I have to get something from the kitchen," said Charles. "I'll be right back."

Julia remembered the chocolate and the two rolls she had bought from Mrs. Tammen. She broke the chocolate in two and put it on the table. Next to that she put one roll for each of them. That would be their lunch.

Charles crawled back through the opening, holding his bottle filled with cocoa. He smiled when he saw the chocolate and the rolls.

"Here," he said, and handed Julia the baby bottle. The nipple was new, just like hers at home. She drank from it. Then Charles drank from it, and then she did again.

"Listen," Julia said, "let's pretend we're grown up. You're the husband and I'm the wife."

"Okay," said Charles. He sat up straight, with a very serious face, and didn't say a word.

"You're supposed to say something," whispered Julia.

"What?" asked Charles.

"I don't know."

Charles couldn't think of anything. "Let's watch TV," he said finally.

"Hmm," said Julia.

"Turn on the TV," said Charles. Julia stood up. She was about to pretend she was turning on the TV, then stopped.

"No," she said. "Do it yourself." And she sat down.

They were pretending to be grown-ups, looking serious. Julia looked into Charles' eyes. She stared hard, and he stared back. They tried to stare each other down, until Charles laughed and gave up, and they were Charles and Julia again.

Julia took the photograph of Oma out of the shopping bag.

"It was taken on the first day of school," Julia said. The picture showed Julia standing with her backpack and her lunch bag, holding Oma's hand.

"She always took you to school and picked you up when you first started school," said Charles.

"How did you know that?" asked Julia.

"We go to the same school, remember?"

Julia remembered that Charles often used to walk behind her, but she had never paid any attention to him. Well, that was when he was Chubby, not Charles. She'd never paid any attention to him before today, at least not really.

"Does your Oma always cook lunch for you?" asked Charles.

"Usually."

"I never knew my grandmother," Charles told her. "She died before I was born." Then he asked, "Do you ever think about what things were like before you were born?"

Julia thought and said, "No."

"Me neither, but my mother and father always tell me what a great cook my grandmother was," said Charles. "Sometimes my mother makes things she learned to cook from Grandma."

"So when you're eating, it's as if your grandma were still there," said Julia.

"No," said Charles. "Not for me. I can't imagine my grandmother, or what she looked like."

"Oh," said Julia.

"Does your Oma help you with your homework?" asked Charles.

"She does sometimes," said Julia.

"She will again soon," said Charles.

"You think so?" asked Julia. "If you could've seen Oma lying in her bed, looking so weird. But she did snore, a little. I *know* I heard her."

"I'm sure you did," said Charles. "You . . . you really love your Oma, don't you?"

"Yes," said Julia.

They sat there in silence, staring at Oma's photograph. Charles' legs were beginning to cramp. He stood up and gave Julia the baby bottle. She drank a little and handed it back to Charles.

Suddenly they both heard footsteps overhead.

Charles stood there, frozen to the spot.

"I think it's my big brother," he whispered.

Julia looked at the brick door. It was closed tight. Nobody would think of looking for them here, as long as they didn't make a sound.

# Chapter Nine

Julia and Charles sat facing each other, listening to the footsteps. *Tap, tap, tap.* Back and forth, back and forth. Then silence. Julia was about to say something when the footsteps started up again. They heard the door open. Someone was going down the steps. *Tap, tap, tap.*

Charles turned off the flashlight. They listened to the sound of the footsteps fading away. Something crackled in the backyard.

They waited in the dark, not saying anything for a long time.

"Phew," breathed Charles, and turned on the flashlight. Julia saw relief in his face. The tension had made Julia forget Oma. But now her worries were back again. Julia saw the image clearly: Oma lying in her bed, so white and old.

"Are you thinking about her again?"

"Yes," whispered Julia. She was glad Charles guessed what she was thinking about. Julia wanted to tell him more about Oma, but she could only smile.

"Why are you smiling?" asked Charles. They were still whispering. It's our whispering cave, Julia thought happily.

"Sometimes when I'm in bed with Oma, she reads to me," said Julia.

"Nobody ever reads to me," Charles said.

"I don't really sleep with Oma," Julia said quietly. "I have my own room. But every once in a while when I don't like my room, I go barefoot to Oma's room and snuggle next to her in her big double bed. Oma says I lie where my grandfather used to lie."

"But you have cold feet," said Charles.

"Why?"

"Because you go to your Oma's room barefoot."

"Oh, yes! But they warm up quickly. Anyway, when Oma turns, the bed groans."

"Why?"

"Because Oma weighs a lot. A groaning bed with a snoring Oma." Julia giggled and went on. "I inch over to her, and Oma picks up her glasses from the night table and puts them on her nose. Then she gets the big red Hans Christian Andersen book off the shelf over the bed. The bed keeps groaning. Oma usually reads to me out of that book. I know all the stories almost by heart. Sometimes Oma cheats. She tries to make a story shorter because she's tired. But I know it right away. You can't make the story shorter, I tell her. So Oma reads on, but she keeps asking me, 'Aren't you tired yet?' 'No,' I say, and I keep listening. Then I turn onto my back and look up at the ceiling light. There are always a couple of dead flies in the glass shade. Oma keeps reading until I fall asleep next to her, but I always wake up in my own bed the next morning."

"Does she carry you to your room?" asked Charles.

"Yes. Oma's pretty strong."

"You know," said Charles softly, "your grandmother must like it too, when you go to her room, because your grandfather isn't alive anymore and there's nobody to lie next to her except you."

"Oma said that too," said Julia.

"Don't your parents yell at you when you fall asleep in her bed?"

"No—what is there to yell about?"

Charles sighed. "I think your parents yell at you much less than mine do. And you have Oma. Tell me more about her."

"Why?"

"Because I don't have an Oma. You know, when you talk about her, I can pretend what it would be like to have a grandma." Charles sat his old rag doll next to him.

Julia looked at Charles, and she suddenly realized that she liked him. She realized she wasn't sitting with him because she had nothing better to do. She wanted to be with him.

I think he likes me, too. Maybe he could be my friend, she thought.

But then Jacob would be angry. Besides, Jacob and everybody else thinks Charles is dumb. What am I going to do?

Her head was spinning with thoughts about Oma, Charles, Jacob, and everybody else when Charles said, "Say something."

"No—I'm thinking about something," said Julia.

"About what?"

"I can't tell you."

"Then tell me more about your grandmother, okay?"

"Okay."

# Chapter Ten

They sat in their whispering cave under the porch and talked. Every once in a while they stopped to listen for approaching footsteps. It was a little chilly. But talking and being together warmed them both. Julia told Charles about the things she had done with her grandmother.

Charles felt as if he were doing the things

with them. It was almost as if Oma were his, too.

Julia was telling him about the times she needed Oma most. "When there's a thunderstorm, Oma *has* to be with me," she said. "I know it's dumb, but I'm really afraid of storms. You're not supposed to be afraid—"

Charles interrupted, "My dad says that too. He's always explaining to me that the storm clouds have an electrical charge, and that it's the electricity you see as lightning. The heat of the electricity makes the air expand with a loud noise. It goes *boom*, and that's thunder."

"My mother explained it to me, too," said Julia. "But I'm still afraid. I'm so afraid, I shake like this."

She acted out her trembling for Charles. He trembled with her until they both started laughing.

"What do you and Oma do when there's a storm?" asked Charles.

"She comforts me. But mostly she's just there with me. Not always, though. One time it was really bad," Julia told him. "There was a storm with thunder and lightning. I thought the whole world was falling apart. I was alone in the house when there was a loud *boom.* My parents were on their way home, and Oma was away."

"You were scared, huh?" said Charles.

"Was I ever! I hid in my closet. There's just enough room for me there. I pushed myself way back into my dresses, but I left the closet door open a tiny bit and plugged my ears with my fingers."

"Did that help?" asked Charles.

"No! I pretended the closet was a rocket ship, and I was flying the rocket above the storm. That didn't help either. The storm and the noise were too strong. But then I heard somebody calling me. . . ."

"Oma?" asked Charles.

"Yes. She had come home because she didn't want me to be alone."

"Was she surprised when you came out of the closet?" asked Charles.

"No, because she knows I hide there sometimes."

"Did she go into the closet with you?"

"No, it's not big enough. 'Come with me,' she said, and we went into the bathroom, where she dried her wet hair. I didn't even hear the storm anymore."

"When you're with Oma, it's quiet, even if it's really loud," said Charles.

"That's right," said Julia. "Oma filled the tub with warm water, and the bathroom got all steamed up."

Julia was happy thinking about it. "When Oma is with me," she said, "I'm allowed to use as much water as I want."

"My parents always say a full tub is wasteful," said Charles.

"Mine do too," Julia told him. "But not Oma. She knows that if you fill it halfway, it's not an ocean. We ran a whole ocean of water into the tub, and I got in and played ship in the storm. Oma sat on the rim of the bathtub pretending to be the storm. The soap dish was the ship.

"I was rocking in the water like crazy, and Oma was blowing. The waves got higher and higher. But in spite of the storm, the ship landed on Knee Island. Then it tipped over, and the whole crew fell into the sea. But they were all saved. Oma ran out of breath. She groaned and went, 'Phew, I'm not so young anymore.' And I said, 'You're sixty-eight.' And Oma asked me, 'Do you really know how old that is?' "

"Well, it's just sixty-eight," said Charles.

"That's what I said," said Julia. "So Oma

showed me with a yardstick how old that is. There are thirty-six inches on the yardstick. The thirty-six inches are her whole life, she said. Oma pointed at the thirty-two-inch mark and said, 'About this much of my life is already over.' I could see that it wasn't very far to the end of the yardstick. Just this much farther."

Julia held up her hands about four inches apart. "Then Oma pointed to the thirty-four-inch mark and said, 'Maybe I've gotten this far. Or maybe only up to here,' and she pointed to twenty-six inches. 'Any of those could be sixty-eight years,' Oma said.

"After that Oma and I didn't want to talk anymore. That was the first time I ever thought that Oma was going to die someday. I was very sad—and scared.

"Then Oma wrapped me up in a big towel. The towel was soft. But Oma's hands are rough. You can feel them through the cloth.

"When Mama and Daddy came home, they saw that half of the ocean had spilled onto the bathroom floor."

"They always show up when they shouldn't," said Charles.

"Exactly," said Julia. "Mama yelled at us about the mess on the floor. But Oma told her, 'That's no mess, that's half the ocean.' You should have seen them stare at her." Julia imitated her parents' stare. "Daddy said it was lucky that Oma was my grandmother and not my mother. He said Oma was much stricter with him when he was little.

"So then Oma gave a little speech. She admitted that she had been much stricter with Daddy than she is with me. Oma said she had been too strict with Daddy because she wasn't really grown up herself when he was little. She told my parents that she had been about the same age as they were, and that at that age you get upset too easily and don't know what's important. But now she knew, and that's why she wasn't so strict anymore. Then Oma said something else."

Julia smiled.

"Tell me," Charles demanded.

" '*She* is important,' Oma said, pointing to me. 'You have to play with her and do silly things with her. That's important. And this'—Oma pointed at the water on the floor—'this is not important. It can be wiped up. But you'll learn that too,' said Oma. My parents went out of the bathroom shaking their heads."

"Were they angry?" asked Charles.

"Annoyed, I guess, but they do love my Oma. Oma got a rag and gave me one, and we wiped half the ocean up off the bathroom floor."

"Oh, boy," said Charles. "I would have liked to have a grandmother like that."

"You can visit me when she's well again," said Julia. Julia realized she really meant it—she wasn't saying it to be polite.

"I will," said Charles. "I hope she gets better soon."

# Chapter Eleven

Charles put his frayed rag doll back in the shoe box. It was hard to tell that once she had been white. There were only a few brown yarn hairs left on her head.

"I don't want her to get cold," said Charles, and covered her with a newspaper. "I used to take her to bed with me. I couldn't sleep without her. I used to hold her in my arms and tell her things. In the morning when I woke up, she'd be lying somewhere else—next to my bed or by my feet. I always thought she went for walks at night."

"Why don't you take her to bed with you now?" asked Julia. "You can hide her under the blankets. Then nobody would find her, and nobody would laugh at you."

"No," said Charles. "*Someone* would find her in my room. I can visit her down here anytime I want to."

Julia ate the rest of her chocolate and her roll. It was nice being with Charles. Julia sighed. It was nicer than being with Jacob. Jacob only wanted to do silly stuff and be tough. The things she and Charles did together wouldn't have interested him at all. And he wasn't as good a listener, either.

"Are you thinking about your Oma?" asked Charles. Julia shook her head. She desperately wanted to know what was wrong with Oma, but at the same time she was afraid to find out.

"I have to go home," she said.

Charles took two bricks out of the wall and looked out. There was nobody around, so they moved the rest of the bricks and crawled out, closing up the opening.

Charles' bicycle was in the backyard, leaning against the wall. "Wow! A five-speed!" exclaimed Julia. "Can I ride it?"

"Sure," said Charles.

Julia hung her shopping bag on the handlebars and rode several times around the yard, then around Charles. First with two hands, then with one.

"Want me to ride you home?" asked Charles when Julia braked to a stop.

"Yes, I'd like that," said Julia.

They biked out of the yard. Julia held on to the seat, but that didn't work too well, so she held on to Charles.

Too bad he doesn't have a handle on his back to hang on to, thought Julia. She giggled at the thought, imagining Charles with a handle on his back.

As they rode past Jacob's house, Julia pressed herself closer to Charles' back. She was almost hiding, although she didn't really mean to. Julia thought, I can ride a bike with anyone I feel like.

Then Julia thought of Oma, lying there with her sharp nose and her pale face.

"Turn left," she cried. Charles turned left. "Now right," she ordered. Charles obeyed. "Stop," she yelled. Charles braked in front of a big house with a garden full of roses. There was a sign on the house: DR. SCHMITT, GENERAL PRACTITIONER. He was Oma's doctor.

"Will you wait for me?" asked Julia.

"Sure," said Charles.

Julia went up to the sign and read: OFFICE HOURS 8–12 AND 4–6:30.

The office was closed, but Julia had to talk

to the doctor. Go ahead! Ring the bell! she told herself.

If the doctor should come out and ask, "What do you want?" Julia would tell him.

Julia pictured a big scowling man in a white smock.

She went back down the path. "I didn't ring the bell," she said to Charles. "It's not office hours."

"I wouldn't have either," said Charles.

"Come on," said Julia. "I want to see how Oma is."

"Maybe she's not lying in bed that way anymore," said Charles hopefully.

Charles pedaled hard to Julia's house. When they got there, Julia grabbed her shopping bag and ran past the linden tree into the house.

"Wait for me!" Julia yelled over her shoulder.

Charles nodded okay.

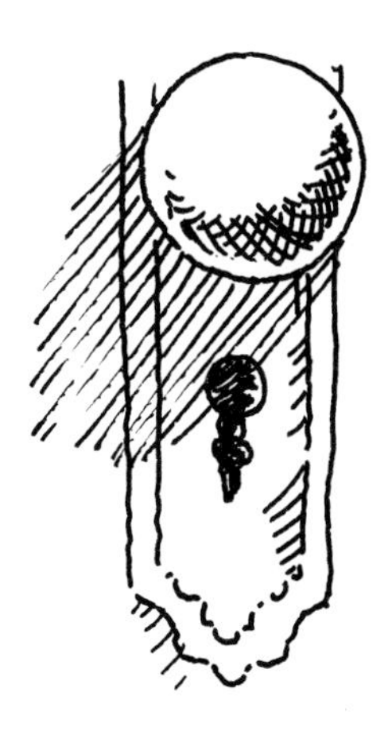

# Chapter Twelve

"Oma?" Julia called softly from downstairs. But there was no answer. Oma must still be asleep. Julia dropped the shopping bag, with Oma's picture in it, in the kitchen and rushed upstairs. She stopped at the door and listened.

She desperately wanted to hear a tiny snore coming out of the room—just one.

But she didn't hear anything. All she could see through the keyhole was darkness.

Had Oma really snored before? Or had Julia imagined it? Julia was afraid to open the door and go inside. What if she couldn't wake Oma? What if Oma never snored again?

Julia decided she didn't want to know now. Not while she was alone in the house.

Julia ran downstairs and looked out the front window. The linden tree stood there as always, big and green. A car drove past. It wasn't her mother's—Julia could tell by the sound of the motor. But where was Charles?

The house felt so big and gloomy, so silent. Julia felt she couldn't wait here for her parents alone inside. She rushed out into the yard and into the sun.

She gave a sigh of relief when she saw Charles' legs dangling from a low branch of the linden tree. Grabbing a branch, she swung up and landed among the branches and leaves next to Charles.

"Want one?" asked Charles, holding out a cherry. His hand was red from the cherry juice. Julia took the cherry. "It's from your tree," said Charles, grinning.

Julia smiled back at Charles and spat her cherry pit into the yard.

"I listened at the door," she said. "Oma wasn't snoring."

"Did you go into her room?" asked Charles.

"No," said Julia. "I was too scared."

They climbed down from the tree.

"Waiting for my parents is dumb," said Julia. "Let's ride your bike."

"Okay," said Charles.

"It's my turn to pedal," said Julia.

Julia biked fast. She liked that Charles held on to her shoulders. Somehow it felt comforting to have him sitting behind her.

# Chapter Thirteen

Suddenly Jacob loomed in front of them. He spread his arms like a traffic cop, and ordered, "Stop!"

Julia didn't stop. She rode past Jacob. Jacob saw Charles—Charles holding on to Julia's shoulders!

I can't believe this, thought Jacob.

He was furious. "You fatso!" he yelled, and started to run after them. That fatso can't ride with Julia! he thought. He's holding on to Julia!

Jacob stopped running. "Fatso has a crush, Fatso has a crush," he yelled over and over.

Although he was yelling at Charles, Jacob was really furious with Julia.

"Chubby and Julia are going steady!" yelled Jacob at the top of his lungs, his face turning tomato red.

"What do you care if we're going steady?" Julia yelled back.

Jacob's dumb, Julia thought. It's none of his business. I can be with Charles if I want to.

She knew Jacob wouldn't walk her home from school anymore. At least not if Charles was with her.

Julia was glad they had run into Jacob. It served him right! She wasn't ashamed of being seen together with Charles.

Julia steered the bicycle past the houses at the edge of the field, along the narrow street that led out of town and away from Jacob's yelling. It was the way to the cemetery. She wanted to show Charles something there. It wasn't as big a secret as the whispering cave, but a secret nevertheless.

Why doesn't Charles say something? thought Julia. Jacob must have scared him, she decided.

Julia braked, and they got off the bike. She laid it in the high grass by the wall of the cemetery. Over the wall they could see the tops of some of the gravestones.

Julia sat down next to the bicycle, and Charles sat down next to her.

"Jacob doesn't like me," he said.

"But *why?*" asked Julia.

"Maybe because I'm not in your class," said Charles. "We do the same thing when we see someone from your class. We say to each other, 'Here comes one of the dummies.' " Charles shook his head. "But I think it's something else. I think it's because Jacob likes you. You've always walked to school together. I think he's afraid you're going to walk with me and not with him anymore. Besides, he thinks I'm fat and stupid."

"You're not," said Julia.

Charles didn't say anything. A wasp buzzed around his head. "I think Jacob is jealous," he finally said.

"Hmm," said Julia. He's probably right, she thought.

"We were stupid to run away from him," Charles said. "He couldn't have done anything to us."

"You're right," said Julia.

"Would you walk home from school with me sometimes?" Charles asked, without looking at Julia. He pulled up a blade of grass and swiped at the wasp.

"I might," said Julia. When you share someone's secret place like the whispering cave, thought Julia . . . and when you can talk to someone and they listen to you . . .

and when you have the feeling that you like them . . . then you have a true friend.

Julia looked at Charles and asked, "Do you want to be my friend?"

Charles blushed and nodded.

"Then you have to kiss me," said Julia. Charles turned beet red, but he kissed her—a quick little kiss on the cheek. Then Julia kissed him back.

Now they were really friends. Julia knew it, and Charles knew it too. Charles' face was flushed with happiness.

They sat in the grass next to the bike, feeling a little embarrassed. In the distance they could hear a tractor. Julia could tell by the sound that it wasn't her father's. "Let's go back," Julia said to Charles.

# Chapter Fourteen

Julia stopped at the cemetery gate and turned to Charles. “I want to show you something,” she said. “I’ve never shown it to anyone but Oma.”

Julia and Charles walked through the open iron gate, then along the gravel path, with gravestones on one side and bushes on the other. There was not a soul in sight. Julia stopped in front of a tall wooden cross. "My grandfather's grave," she said.

"Karl Brinkmann," Charles read. "Born in 1901, died in 1975."

"I wasn't even born when my grandfather died," said Julia. "Just like your grandmother and you. Oma and I visit Grandpa a lot. She always tells me about Grandpa, and she waters the flowers on his grave."

"She can't do it now," said Charles.

"But we can," said Julia. They filled the watering can at the main tap, and together they carried the heavy can back to the grave. After they had watered the flowers, Julia bent down by a dense, tall bush that grew next to Grandpa's cross and waved to Charles to come closer. As she carefully parted the lower branches, Charles saw a tiny cross. It was made of two pieces of wood, and painted blue.

"I made it for my grandfather," said Julia. "Only Oma knows about my cross for

Grandpa. I wanted to give him a present from me."

"It's very nice," said Charles. "My grandfather is over there." Charles pointed to the other side of the cemetery.

"Can you believe there are dead people all around us and under us?"

"And they all used to live in our town," said Charles.

They looked across the cemetery and saw nothing but rows of gravestones, wooden crosses, and motionless dark shrubs glistening in the sun. It was eerie.

Charles said suddenly, "When your Oma dies, she should be buried in the most beautiful spot."

"Where's that?" asked Julia.

Charles looked around. "Over there," he said. "It's warm and sunny. Your Oma would like that."

"No, she wouldn't," said Julia. "Oma likes shady places. I'll show you."

They ran out of the cemetery and up a hill covered with bushes and birch trees.

They stood at the top of the hill, looking down at the cemetery and the town and across the fields to the woods. "This is Oma's favorite spot," said Julia. "It's shady under the trees, but still enough sunshine gets through."

"I like it here too," said Charles.

Julia sat down on a cushion of moss. She felt as if she were sitting in a green easy chair. She pulled up her legs and looked toward town. Charles sat down next to her.

"I think when your Oma dies, everyone will come to her funeral," he said.

"I'll make a tiny cross for her, the way I did for my grandfather," said Julia. She lay down in the moss and blinked into the sunlight through the birch leaves. Then she closed her eyes and lay completely still. Like Oma, she thought.

Charles tickled her nose with a blade of

grass. Julia opened her eyes. "I don't think Oma would like to be buried here," she said.

"Why not?"

"Because Oma would want to be buried next to my grandfather."

"You're probably right," said Charles.

Julia pointed to the wooden bridge crossing the narrow stream a couple of hundred yards on their left. "See that bridge?" she said.

"What about it?" asked Charles.

"One time Oma crossed it when the water was very high. Daddy and I saw her do it."

"That's dangerous," said Charles.

"But Oma wanted to. She crossed it even though Daddy told her not to. The water was gurgling right under the bridge. Just as Oma reached the middle of the bridge, there was a loud *crack* and the bridge broke. And there was Oma, lying in the water—it was pretty deep and cold, and Oma doesn't know how to swim. Her wide skirt was floating on top of the water and she was paddling like crazy with one hand. You know what she was holding in the other?"

"No, what?"

"Her bag. She was yelling for Daddy to save her handbag first, because there was a lot of money in it. Oma was yelling, and Daddy was pulling."

"Her handbag?"

"No, silly, both. Oma wouldn't let go of her handbag."

Julia turned and pointed to a path leading into the woods. "Once when we were gathering mushrooms, Oma and I found a huge fossil there. I wanted to take it home, but Oma said we weren't pack donkeys. So we hid the fossil. We hid it so well that we never found it again."

"When your grandmother gets well, let's look for the fossil together," said Charles.

"Yes, let's," said Julia.

They fell silent again. "It is a nice place

to sit, but maybe it wouldn't be nice for Oma," Julia said finally.

"You're right," said Charles. "Oma has to be beside your grandfather."

"I think so too," said Julia. Then she thought of something else. "Do you think Oma will go to Heaven?"

"Oh, sure," said Charles. "It's very nice there—even nicer than here." Then he asked, "Where do you suppose Heaven is?"

"Heaven must be beyond the clouds," Julia said, looking up at the blue sky dotted with little white clouds. "I hope it's nothing like the land of milk and honey, where there's nothing to do. That wouldn't be good for my Oma—Oma needs to be busy all the time."

"Maybe she'd keep the place tidy," said Charles, grinning.

"No, I don't think it would be the right place for her," said Julia. "But I don't want to think about it. I want Oma to be here with me. Someday I'll ask her what she thinks Heaven is like."

They watched a yellow butterfly flutter in between the light-green birch leaves. "Maybe it comes from Heaven," said Charles.

"Don't be silly," said Julia. "Butterflies can't fly that far."

Julia thought of the many times she had come here with Oma. She thought about the time they had eaten pork chops and drunk lemonade, and the time they had cleaned the mushrooms they had gathered. "You know, Charles," Julia said, "everywhere I look I remember something Oma and I did together—here, by the river, in the woods, in the cemetery, at home. Everywhere."

The more Julia thought of Oma, the sadder and more uneasy she became. She jumped up. She was feeling restless. But the main reason she got up was that she didn't want Charles to see she was crying.

# Chapter Fifteen

They took a shortcut back to town through a field, bouncing more than riding.

"Stop," Charles shouted suddenly. He wanted to share something else with Julia. He pointed to a spot at the curb next to a street lamp not far from his house. "This is where I found my dog. He was run over."

"I didn't know you had a dog," said Julia. "When did it happen?"

"A year ago," Charles told her softly. "I was alone in the house when I heard tires squealing real loud; then I heard a car drive away. I didn't think anything of it. Anyway, some time later I called Timo. Timo was my dog's name. I wanted to play with him, but he didn't come. So I went outside to look for him, and that's when I found him—lying there in the gutter. His legs were tucked in, and there was blood on his nose. I kept stroking him, hoping he would move. Then I looked into his eyes and saw that he was dead. Dead! I remembered that awful squealing of tires, and I kept thinking I could have saved him, that it was my fault he was lying there so still. I picked up Timo and carried him into the garden."

Charles took Julia's hand and led her to the back of the house. They stopped by a little wooden cross in front of a bush. It looked like Julia's cross for her grandfather.

"I made it for Timo," said Charles. "I laid

him down on the ground and got a shovel. But I couldn't bury him.

"When my parents came home, Dad dug a deep hole; then he wrapped Timo in his blanket and buried him. My mother cried, and I did too. You know, Julia," said Charles, "I didn't really feel anything then. I don't think I understood that Timo was dead. I said it, but I couldn't believe it. That took a few days. Then I really missed him."

Julia and Charles stood there looking at the little wooden cross.

"I wanted to show you Timo's grave," said Charles, feeling a strange lump in his throat.

"What kind of dog was he?" Julia asked.

"A mutt. We had such great times together. Timo liked to grab my socks and pull them off my feet. He would pull them off and run away, and I was supposed to catch him. I taught him a whole bunch of stuff. I loved him a lot. I was never afraid at night when he was with me."

I like Charles a lot, thought Julia. Then she thought of Oma again, and how she lay there in her bed. “Listen,” said Julia, “I’ve got to get home.”

“Do you want me to come with you?” asked Charles.

“I’d like that,” said Julia.

# Chapter Sixteen

Charles held on to Julia as they rode along the street to Julia's house. Julia could see the gate was open and the tractor inside the yard. Daddy was home!

I hope Oma isn't still lying there so sharp and white, Julia thought.

When they stopped at the front door, she jumped off the bike and tore through the open door. Charles ran after her.

"Daddy!" she screamed. But there was no answer.

"He must be upstairs with Oma. Come on!" They raced up the stairs.

Just before she reached Oma's door, Julia suddenly stopped. Charles didn't stop as fast, and he bumped into her. Julia stood there listening. There was not a sound.

Carefully Julia turned the doorknob and slowly opened the door a crack.

Oma was almost sitting up in bed. She had two pillows stuffed behind her back, her face was less pale, and her nose wasn't so sharp anymore. She looked at Julia curiously.

"Hey," said Oma, "why are you sneaking in here?"

"Oma, you—What's wrong with you?" Julia blurted out.

"Oh, nothing," said Oma. "The doctor says it's my circulation. Nuts."

"Nuts? The doctor?" Julia came closer to Oma.

"No, child, my circulation. That's why I get dizzy spells. I didn't feel well this morning. I had to stay in bed and take medicine. I must have overslept."

Suddenly Julia felt so lighthearted, she could have flown around the room. Instead, she sat on the edge of the bed and said, "I came in to see you after school. You were lying there so still. I was really scared, and I thought you . . ."

Julia didn't want to tell her what she had thought. Oma looked at Julia and stroked her hair. "You must have thought I was dead," she said.

"Uh-huh," said Julia. "But when I was leaving your room, I thought I heard a little snore."

"Me? Snore!" said Oma. "I never snore!"

"How do you know?" asked Julia. "You

can't hear yourself when you're sleeping. A snoring Oma!"

"Hey!" said Oma, laughing. "Don't get fresh with an old lady. No, my little chick, I'm not going to die soon. This tough old bird is not about to fly away."

Oma looked past Julia toward the door. Charles was standing there, unsure whether to come in or not.

"Isn't that Chubby?" asked Oma.

"No, Charles," corrected Julia. She realized she had completely forgotten he was there. "He's going to visit us a lot from now on," said Julia, "because he doesn't have an Oma."

"Oh? So you're going to divide me up between you," said Oma.

Charles came into the room and stood next to the bed.

"Is this your friend?" asked Oma.

"Yes," Julia and Charles said at the same time.

"My goodness," said Oma, surprised. "How very nice." Then she sighed and said, "But I do feel tired and need some rest now."

"Go back to sleep," said Julia, smoothing Oma's covers. "Do you need anything?"

"Just rest, dear."

"I'll see you later, Oma," said Julia. She closed the door as quietly as possible.

Charles and Julia ran down the stairs and down the hall, grabbing cherries off the bureau. Julia popped a couple into her mouth, and Charles did the same.

They raced out of the house and into the yard. Julia swung herself up into the linden tree and started climbing. Charles came right behind her.

They sat high up in the tree, eating cherries and spitting the pits down to the ground. I am so happy, thought Julia. If Oma hadn't gotten sick, Charles and I would never have become friends.

Julia looked toward the barn and saw her father coming toward them. "Do you have any cherry pits left?" she asked.

Charles stuck out his tongue—it held his last cherry pit. Julia had one in her mouth too.

Her father was just about under the linden tree when Julia yelled, "Now!" and they spat the pits down.

Her father's surprised face stared up at them, then slowly the surprise turned into a smile, and he began to laugh.